I Love Mud
and
Mud Loves Me

Written by Vicki Stephens
Pictures by Rowan Barnes-Murphy

SCHOLASTIC INC.

New York   Toronto   London   Auckland   Sydney

Copyright © 1994 by Scholastic Inc.
All rights reserved. Published by Scholastic Inc.
Printed in the U.S.A.
ISBN 0-590-27381-7

2 3 4 5 6 7 8 9 10   09   00 99 98 97 96 95 94

3

5

ISBN 0-590-27381-7

90000>

EAN

9 780590 273817

SCHOLASTIC INC.

STAGE A

The Birthday Present

by Mavis Smith

EE

SCHOLASTIC

THIS BOOK IS THE PROPERTY OF:

STATE _____

PROVINCE _____

COUNTY _____

PARISH _____

SCHOOL DISTRICT _____

OTHER _____

Book No. _____

Enter information in spaces to the left as instructed.

ISSUED TO	Year Used	CONDITION	
		ISSUED	RETURNED
_____	_____	_____	_____
_____	_____	_____	_____
_____	_____	_____	_____
_____	_____	_____	_____
_____	_____	_____	_____
_____	_____	_____	_____
_____	_____	_____	_____
_____	_____	_____	_____

PUPILS to whom this textbook is issued must not write on any page or mark any part of it in any way, consumable textbooks excepted.

1. Teachers should see that the pupil's name is clearly written in ink in the spaces above in every book issued.
2. The following terms should be used in recording the condition of the book: New; Good; Fair; Poor; Bad.